WINNER OF THE 1995 3-DAY
NOVEL WRITING CONTEST

I called Mat the next morning. She
wasn't home, so I ranted at her answering machine instead, "Hey Mat, this is
Lena. Just thought you should know
we are flat fucking *fucked* in my opinion. Worked on a story called "Everything In The Night" all day yesterday
and wound up with a whole eighteen
pages—four of which have been burned for good cause. That makes it about
twelve manuscript pages. That's in
twelve hours and change. That would be
a goddamned page an hour. How in the
hell do we think we're going to do a hundred or so pages in seventy-two hours?"

Body SPEaking Words

LOREE HARRELL

ANVIL PRESS

Cover design by JT Osborne
Illustrations by Nicky Rickard

Printed and bound in Canada
First Edition

Canadian Cataloguing in Publication Data

Harrell, Loree, 1960-
Body speaking words
ISBN 1-895636-09-4
I. Title
PS3558.A62499B62 1996   813'.54   C96-910380-8

Represented in Canada by the Literary Press Group
Distributed by General Distribution Services

Anvil Press
Suite 204A—175 East Broadway,
Vancouver, BC
Canada   V5T 1W2

Respectfully dedicated to all of you
with stories to tell and the courage to
tell them; and to all of you with
hearts to listen.

When I was eleven, Grandma read me some stories from her journal.

SATURDAY

Mat is here with me today. And yesterday. And tomorrow. Locked up in a small room with three dogs and two computers in a cabin by the river. Mat is good. As a writer. As a friend. As someone to be there when things are hard. As someone to laugh with on the other side of hard. Someone who understands that the insanity is usually temporary.

Mat and I stocked up for the long weekend. Dark chocolate raspberry sticks, ginger animal cookies, lemon poppyseed muffins, and bananas in the bathroom corner by the toilet, coffee plugged in next to the toothpaste, beer and cream soda in the cooler on the landing outside the bathroom door. Real food in the main house—nothing that requires more cooking than three minutes of radiation.

This weekend is the first time Mat and I have really spent together. We met a month ago in a writing workshop over on the coast, had coffee together once, had beer together twice, and here we sit in the middle of 72 hours of writing. Straight through. With each of us to be holding a novel, ready for transcription, on the other end.

We thought it would be fun.

Right now, both of us believe we're insane. Certifiably and verifiably.

I started this. Saw a competition in Writer's Market two weeks ago: Best Novel Written Over The Labour Day Weekend. Thought, what the fuck, I do marathon, that sounds like fun. Mentioned it off-hand to Mat at our Thursday night Pond Scum Writers' group. Mat said, "Cool!"

I said, "I'm calling to have information faxed to me tomorrow. I'll give you a call when I get it in case you want to play."

Mat said, "Great. Sounds like fun."

Well it *did* sound like fun. When the fax came I got all excited and decided immediately to do it. Called and said to Mat, "So this is the deal. Start midnight Friday, end midnight Monday. All writing to be done in that time frame. A couple days to transcribe it after that. Notes and outlines allowed in advance for those anal types that use notes and outlines. Fifteen bucks to enter, winner announced Halloween night. You in?"

Mat got all excited. "I'm in."

I get that Mat and I are possibly a bit too much alike. Not a helluva lot of balance here.

Go directly to bliss. Do not pass "Go." And fuck the money.

We spent a couple of days each being all excited about doing the Write A Novel In Three Days thing. Told all our friends. Didn't tell any of the other Pond Scum so we could surprise them with our Astounding Accomplishment at our party the Friday after Labour Day. Laughed at all those Other People taking ten years to write a novel. Laughed at ourselves for being insane enough to do this. Agreed that, of course, in three days the novel had to be a piece of shit— couldn't possibly expect otherwise. Agreed that this was a great way to just get that pesky first novel done and out of the way and get to work on the second one.

Then, a couple of days after those couple of days, I settled back into my writing. Other stuff. Thought I'd crank out a short story. Went out on the deck to do my Naked Writer In The Sun thing and started the next short story with a great first sentence.

There are things we cannot afford to treat
as ordinary in this life.

It tailed out, dead-ended, and died inside of four pages.

Maybe a great first sentence, but not in the direction I wrote it.

Annoying, but no big deal. I took a break and read a story in *Glimmer Train*, was absolutely knocked over by the voice and power in this little six page story, started a new story with a new great first sentence and wrote for another six hours.

I want to tell you a story about a man I never met.

Decent-to-good stuff. Eleven pages. Writing book pages. Handwritten writing book pages. 1.65 of which equal one manuscript page.

Got a request to join my housemates and their company for dinner. Usually don't break in the middle of a piece, but figured I'd better get used to doing that if I was going to write longer stuff. Besides, I was hungry.

Went into the house. Not time yet, so talked for ten minutes and went back out to the cabin to write for another half hour. Couldn't get back in. That strong voice that had been so consistent for six hours and twelve pages was gone. Said fuck it (a lot of that lately) and went back to eat.

Spent four more hours after dinner trying to get the story back. Found two fatal flaws in the first paragraph right off the bat. Finally re-found the voice after two hours. Realized by midnight that the entire story bore no relationship to the original premise. Went to bed. Fourteen pages plus the four in the trash. Eighteen handwritten writing notebook pages in thirteen hours.

I called Mat the next morning. She wasn't home, so I ranted at her answering machine instead, "Hey Mat, this is Lena. Just thought you should know we are flat fucking *fucked* in my opinion. Worked on a story called "Everything In The Night" all day yesterday and wound up with a whole eighteen pages—four of which have been burned for good cause. That makes it about twelve manuscript pages.

That's in *twelve hours* and change. That would be a god-damned page an hour. How in the *hell* do we think we're going to do a hundred or so pages in seventy-two hours?"

Mat called back later, laughing. "Hey, Lee! Got your message, it . . ."

I clicked Talk and said, "Hi Mat, I'm here."

"Oh hi! Got your message, it was hysterical."

I was in a slightly calmer, more accepting space now. Said, "You have an odd sense of humour, given that you are soon to be locked up in a small room with me and given that deadlines make me fucking crazy. Particularly physically impossible ones. How the hell many pages are *you* writing in a day now?"

Mat said, "Anywhere from four to sixteen in three to twelve hours."

More than me. Damn.

I said, "Well those numbers *still* don't work. How the hell are we going to do this? I'm assuming we're going to need to sleep in there somewhere. Maybe shower. Christ, I don't even know what I'm writing about yet!" I was feeling substantially less smug about those Other People who were busily creating outlines and notes now. And probably had been for the past three months.

Mat said, "We'll be fine, Lee. Just gonna sit down and keep our fingers moving until we're done. It's not like we're expecting it to be good or anything—we already agreed it would be shit by definition!" Mat was still annoyingly cheery. One of the things I like about Mat is she carries a good dose of Kali dark. Perky drives me nuts most days.

Finished "Everything In The Night" after working on it good hunks of three days. Eleven manuscript pages. Damn story fought me every inch of the way. Dumped the great first sentence and the first two pages in the process.

A hundred pages in three days. Yeah, right.

Children are surrogate dogs.

So Mat planned to come out early Friday. Settle in, devise our strategy, take a nap before midnight, like that. I planned to not have anything to do Friday but sleep and wait for one of the sentences on the wall to pop out as The First Sentence.

Right.

I woke up at 6:30 Friday morning after going to sleep about five hours earlier. Ran all day—errands, sign loan papers, clean, business calls, chop up enough raw beef heart to get the dog through the weekend. Thought about paying the bills but dumped that as extraneous bullshit. No money anyway. Never got a nap.

Mat showed up with her two dogs, the dogs that she hadn't wanted to bring because they would be distracting, at about 10:30 p.m. We had time to unload her car, smoke a couple cigarettes, and let her read about half the words on the wall before it was midnight, time to start.

SATURDAY

*A thousand words died when John's two
fingers got caught in the press.*

There are about sixty slips of paper taped to the walls
of the cabin. Sixty slips of paper with first sentences, bits of
overheard conversations, story ideas, words that sparkle,
images that dazzle, and assorted therapeutic drivel. I
robbed my idea file for anything that might be useful, on
the theory that one would stand out as The First Sentence,
that any time I got stuck I could just look up at the ceiling,
or walk over to the wall, and grab something to get going
again.

Good theory.

The First Sentence never appeared.

So at one minute after midnight, I decided to play first-
sentence-tarot instead. Grounded and centred. Well, not
really, but grounded and centred as much as was possible
given my total lack of grounded and centred-ness. Invoked
Spirit and Guides to stand with me. The invocation was a
bit on the wimpy side. Energy a little low. Bottom line was
I just wanted to sleep. Shuffled all my little index cards,
laid them out in a medicine wheel on the bed. The centre
card, The First Sentence, was one I really liked.

*I woke in a tent, wet from dreams
of caramel apples and sex.*

13

Fought that first sentence for two hours. Didn't get more than two paragraphs in any direction.

Figured it was a sentence about camping. Which took me right back into a story about Elk Lake I wrote a couple weeks ago. Didn't want to write a camping story. Certainly not that one. Let it tail out.

Decided it was a sentence about waking up in a circus tent. After four sentences it was very clear I didn't have any interest in writing a hundred pages about waking up in a circus tent. I didn't believe the main character. Let it tail out.

And so, again, this goes nowhere and takes me along with it. I would say it's just a bum first line, except that I've started with worse—oh, shit like "The lettuce flew out of 17F and landed at my feet"—and wound up with stories I like. So I get that this is not the fault of the sentence, but a flaw in the receptor. Hopefully temporary.

Pap is a function of the state of the receptor,
not the veracity of the content.

Scanned for other kinds of available tents. Oxygen tent? Set it in a hospital nursery, write the stories all those little premature babies have to tell. Don't think so. Caterpillar tent? Wouldn't fit. Me, that is. My body wouldn't fit in a caterpillar tent. Unless I wrote some sort of surrealistic sci-fi thing with huge tent caterpillars—or a very small me—on another planet in another dimension. Think I'll

14

pass on that, thank you. Revival tent? Lots of screamin'
hellfire-and-brimstone dialogue. Gosh, just keeps gettin'
better, don't it? Pass.

PAP
Pablum And Poppycock
Precipitous Aggravation of Perspective
Potent Annihilation of Possibility
Patently Atavistic Pollution
Parsimonious Apathetic Puffery

I looked at the clock. 1:30 a.m. The first hour and a half
shot to shit and my brain not getting any sharper. Mat had
been typing away steadily since we started.
I said, "You up for awhile?"
Mat didn't pause in her typing. "Yeah."
"I have to sleep a couple hours. Would you throw some-
thing at me at three?"
Mat glanced over her shoulder at the clock. "Yeah."

I slept under a red and fuschia,
blue and green wool Pendleton blanket,
woke wet from dreams of caramel
apples and sex.
Not necessarily in that order.

15

Mat's voice, her touch on my leg brought me back from dreaming. Brought me back to blink against the light, to try to get my eyes focused. Brought me back to do the impossible again. To attempt it. To see truly if what I have said I wanted is what I want. Brought me back with a little jolt that just right now seems like more pleasure to follow than this absurd idea of writing with no plan, of writing without pause for 72 hours, of writing I don't know what, writing without sleep, until the clock turns past eleven six more times. A little jolt that seems like an infinitely better plan than any of that.

I wake knowing I am scared. Of having nothing to say. Of failing at something I have set myself to. Of spending three days in the company of this woman, this stranger, this friend of less than a month, this person I held warm in my heart from the first time I met her. Warm without cause.

Scared that she can do this better than me. That I won't measure up. Scared at all the rituals, all the writing spaces I have created so painfully for myself, that are now no longer applicable. Given that the core of the ritual is alone.

Out the window. Down the river. Merrily merrily.

Scared mostly that I can't find my body.
Scared that, without my body,
my words are lost to me.

Three dogs are asleep on the floor. There are words plastered all over the ceiling. All over the walls. Words that

were supposed to help. Words I can't see because my eyes
won't focus just yet. May not until my body gets to rest a
couple more long hours.

> *Words slip back into the darkness again,*
> *slip away from my hearing.*
> *I close my eyes to listen,*
> *slip back to the edge of dreaming,*
> *feel the tug of the not-quite-remembered*
> *lost in the waking.*
> *sweet sleep.*
> *The tug of the not-quite-remembered*
> *following me into my waking always.*
> *Never quite remembered other life, other world,*
> *of the night.*
> *And it is always a loss.*
> *The not remembering.*
> *It is always a hard transition to leave that.*
> *To step into waking.*
> *To release the night unknowing.*
> *To walk out into the world*
> *severing the connections*
> *of my body and my soul.*

Mat was still typing away. I tried to type, couldn't see the
screen. Finally settled on scribbling in my notebook.
Didn't have to be able to see to do that. Write in there in

the dark all the time. Kept drifting off every time I closed my eyes to listen for the next sentence.

I looked at the clock. 4:08 and my eyes still hadn't cleared. Head still hadn't cleared. Writing still hadn't cleared. Another hour or so before the birds started calling in the light.

Mat stretched and said, "I have to get some sleep."

I said, "Good. Steve works nights so I'll call him and ask him for a wake-up call at seven." I called, we turned off the lights, left the candles to sputter into darkness on their own. Mat crawled into her sleeping bag, I crawled further down in my bed, the dogs curled up around us, and all slept.

Noctilucent.

That was Friday night into Saturday. This is Saturday. I have to keep reminding myself of where I am in the continuum. Time is already scrambled.

The phone rang at 7:12. Steve with the promised wake-up call. Thanked him, looked over at Mat motionless in her red cocoon on the floor—small black dogs apparently covering all available breathing orifices, wondered briefly if she had been smothered to death, drifted about three minutes, and fell asleep again.

We woke up at 8:34. Not grumpy. Both of us feeling pretty good. Ready to go. I started my day with an

American Spirit straight and guava juice. Mat started hers with hand-rolled Drum and a banana. Sat down to write . . .

The drums demand a price.

When I was eleven, Grandma read me some stories from her journal, some pieces and fragments of her life.

Grandma and I had already had some trouble liking each other by then. She was difficult for me. Easily angered with a cruel edge to her tongue, hugely opinionated, always right, expecting more of me than I believed to be fair at my age. That was also about the time I didn't want to have much to do with family anyway.

One day I was at Grandma's and got stomach-sick when everyone else was going up to the lake to swim and camp overnight. So Grandma stayed home with me. Stayed home, with me grumpy from throwing up instead of being out in the sun by the lake. Me grumpy from not getting to sleep outside in a tent and have *s'mores*, which would have just made me stomach-sick anyway. Always did.

Grandma got tired of listening to my complaints fairly early on in the day. Stood by the side of my bed and said, "So listen, Lena. I am not going to stand here and take the brunt of you being sick. I'm sorry you don't feel well, but that is no cause to take it out on me. I'm going into the other room to read. If you decide you feel well enough to come out and be a human being, then come on out and we can watch some TV or play a game or something. Okay?"

19

I was being a butt and knew it, so I smiled and said, "Okay. I'm sorry, just don't feel very good."

I looked at the pictures of the flying mallards on the wall across from the bed for a while, then drifted back to sleep, and when I woke up I was hungry. Not feeling bad at all anymore. I put on my robe and went out to see what Grandma was doing and if I had already missed lunch. She looked up from the book she was reading by the window, "Feeling better?"

"Lots. I'm sorry for being such a pain before."

Grandma smiled. "Apology accepted. I knew you weren't feeling good, just wasn't about to keep listening to it. I've been sitting here going through some of the writing I've been doing. Let me make you a sandwich if you're hungry—and then we can figure out what we're going to do with our day of freedom from the family."

"I am hungry, thank you," I said. Then, "I didn't know you wrote. What do you write about?"

"Probably nothing very interesting to you. Stories of things that have happened in my life. Stray thoughts. Some little poems."

"Could I hear some of what you've written?"

Grandma looked at me for what seemed like a long time. Long enough that I thought I had maybe asked for something wrong. But then she said, "I would like that. Let me go get you that sandwich and then I'll read a little while you eat."

Grandma read from her three little books all afternoon. Read me stories of a girl younger than me in a place very different. Read stories of falling in love with Grandpa. Of still being in love with Grandpa. Read stories that were just her thinking with her hands. Read stories until we had missed dinner and she called to have a pepperoni pizza delivered so we wouldn't have to stop. Read story after story after story. And all of her stories had poems in their middles. Little poems that were like what she was thinking inside of the story she was telling.

We talked about her stories. Talked about what they meant. We talked about me writing poems. And, after we had eaten the pizza, I went and got my diary out of its secret hidden place in my suitcase and I read her some of what I had written. That was when Grandma started calling me Kavindra when no one else was around. She said that was a Hindu name that meant "mighty poet". That was the night Grandma told me I had stories to tell too.

We stayed up late together that night. Late until Grandma had missed the 11:00 news. Late until I started to get sleepy. And even after I had gone to bed I woke up three times, and the first two times light from the lamp by Grandma's chair was still slipping in underneath my door.

> *Great gift of being together*
> *this showing me*
> *who you are,*
> *who I am*
> *seen through your eyes.*

Grandma seemed different after that night. More like just a real person instead of someone older who was Grandmother. Gentler with me. Smiled sometimes like we were friends who had a secret together. Like we had private jokes that were just ours. Like we knew things about each other that no one else knew. I guess that was true.

I started writing stories around the outsides of my poems. Stories that were like the wrappers around the insides of the poems I was telling.

We don't believe in ordinary things.

Grandma died five years ago. There was no funeral. She didn't want the flowers or the fancy casket or the people weeping over her wax-made face or the fuss and bother. I sat that next day in Grandma's living room, in the middle of the cumulation of eighty years of living, twenty years of traveling. Sat in the middle of fertility gods and Thai dancers, in the middle of fake plastic flowers and the philodendron that had grown all the way around the front window and across the ceiling. Sat on an Indian hassock in front of a teakwood table carved with small Asian people. Listened to the Black Forest cuckoo clock chime the hours, and the halves, and the quarters.

Grandma didn't want me to cry for her. So I honoured her wishes. I cried for me. I cried hard. I could feel in my stomach where Grandma was missing. Where her words

22

were gone from me, where her stories still lived, never-changing. I cried a long time.

Then I felt a touch on my stomach, on my chest. More truly, in my gut, in my heart. The touch made me notice a place in there for Grandma's poems. Made me notice that my heart hurt mostly because it was stretching to fit Grandma's stories in with mine. Stretching to make room for the new stories that were coming, and the old ones to get bigger.

> *I feel your touch gentle on my throat now,*
> *your touch in my gut, in that low place*
> *not stomach, not sex,*
> *your fingers brushing my heart,*
> *and I feel my words,*
> *our words,*
> *open in a clear stream*
> *from my gut*
> *to my heart*
> *to my throat.*
> *I will write them out of my throat*
> *down to my hands for you.*

Mat has been writing steadily. Feel like I have been going in fits and starts. Unclear what I'm writing about, about as far from flow as Cairo is from Dubuque. On the same planet, but that's about all you can say about that.

I have watched this woman. Have tried not to. Have

tried to make sure I am honouring the boundaries of how-ever-she-chooses-to-be-here I have offered. I have remained silent. Have perhaps pulled my body in tighter than I would otherwise. She is beautiful, and more so right now today than when I last saw her. Looks younger, more open. I'm hard-pressed to find that tough person who scared the crap out of me a month ago. That tough person that I wanted to know even though she scared me. Maybe because she scared me.

I can feel in my body where you fit,
even though we've never touched.

I have learned not to run from being scared. Have learned to move toward it, to move toward the danger, toward freedom. I recognized the fear in her almost immediately, embraced it, moved toward it, one more click toward freedom.

Thought I had it handled, thought I'd done a great job. Spent fourteen hours, fourteen precious hours, blinded in the belief it was already handled. Not realizing that I couldn't feel my body. That I had shut down that connection to keep the reach-and-pull from reaching into her space. That connection between me and my body. Between my body and my words.

I can feel my body now. I said out loud to her, "I know."

24

I shoved my words into a quiet marriage with a good man.

I know what is wrong, I know why I have written nine pages of off-track drivel, I know I have shut down my body."

I said, "I'm bringing it back in, so if stuff starts flying around sideways . . ."

She said, ". . . duck."

"Yeah," I said, "duck."

So I can feel my body now. Boy, can I feel my body now. Medium-high hum on all cylinders. This is a good thing. And hard to do in light of thirty-some odd years of learning to turn it off when there are other people around. Until the past couple years, even when the other people around were in my bed. Too much. Too far. Too scared. Too dangerous. There are some things that just stick with you forever. Things that carry a youngness, a part of the not-knowing, brought forward through the learning, burned in deep-hard and engraved in 24-point type in the cells of your body. I've been thinking about those things, wondering if I am still adding new ones not yet known.

So I write. I write because my grandmother wrote. I write because she saw in me back then that I could write and told me so. I write because that is what I have said I will do. Because that is what I have to do. I write to move the ball of words stuck in my throat so I can once again breathe freely for a short while.

My words seemed stuck in my throat forever. Stuck in my throat until at thirteen it was too hard to write them anymore and I started smoking them down, started trying to smoke them down inside. Until at fourteen I started trying to drink them down inside. Until at fifteen I started trying to fuck them down, drug them down. Until next I tried—when all else worked imperfectly to obliterate me—to obliterate the words. Until at eighteen I had to have my throat cut open to let some of my words out. Until at twenty-one, I shoved my words into a quiet marriage to a good man and left them there for twelve years. Tried to shove the words down until, at thirty-two, my grandma died and I started to write them down again, started to speak them a little.

Until fifteen months ago, when a friend saw a couple of my poems, liked them, acknowledged them. Acknowledged me. Gave me "permission to write". And I have written, written a lot. Enough that I can write—can let people read what I've written—without full terror of death. Or of them leaving, which is essentially the same thing. Written enough that now I have to write, that now the words have no patience for waiting in the dark forever. Written enough that the words stuck in my throat are beginning to speak themselves. To know they are welcome.

I am a hurricane in your throat.

Written enough that the stories are bringing other stories, lost stories, with them.

We played strip poker at the garage sale.

When we were thirteen, Karen and I were sitting in Karen's grandmother's garage in the rain. It was a Garage Sale. No garages for sale, but lots of stuff. Knicknacks that had lost their shine, or their meaning, or that Karen's grandmother just didn't want to dust again. A blender that had only one little part not working right. Hardly used other than that. Clothes that no one would ever buy—old lady clothes, housecoats and flowered smocks and poly-ester pants. Old lady jewelry: pink plastic pearls bigger than any oyster ever hatched, coloured glass formed into mosaics of flowers and butterflies and bumblebees, hat pins and tacky cheap cocktail rings. Karen's grandmother wasn't feeling well. Turned out later she was dying. She was inside, confined to her bed. Karen had to go in to check on her every couple hours to see if she needed any food, or help to the bathroom, or more pills.

It had been pouring for some time now, and no one had stopped at the garage sale for hours. I had brought Karen my newest secret to show her. It was a heavy spring with a round handle of red plastic on each end. I'd saved for two months to have $12.95 to send away for it. I ran home from school every day after I ordered it so no one else would get to the mail first in case the package came. That was a close call. The day before it arrived, Mom had stayed home from work and I would have been in big trouble if the package had come that day. It was a Guaranteed Breast Enlarger.

I have been using it faithfully for the past two weeks, three times a day. I keep it hidden in the torn netting under my bed, where my sister and I hide the Oreos and Cheetos we smuggle in from downtown. Every time I use it, I look at the instructions again to make sure I'm doing it right. Squeezing the two round red plastic ends as close together as possible, holding my arms level with my nipples, keeping my elbows down toward the floor, fingers up to the ceiling, to press. Can't yet see that my breasts have enlarged one iota, but I'm hopeful. It is, after all, Guaranteed.

Karen looks at me funny when I show it to her. Doesn't say anything and I get embarrassed. Karen has beautiful breasts, would never need to send $12.95 for two pieces of red plastic, a heavy spring, and a sheet of mimeographed instructions. I never use it again. My breasts never grow any bigger.

We sat there in the garage quiet for quite a while after I showed Karen the Guaranteed Breast Enlarger. Me embarrassed and not seeing anything I could say to take my stupidity away, Karen probably disgusted. We sat there in the quiet in the rain until the twins came by. Dave and Dan were outlaws—smoking, drinking, and doing pot in sixth grade. The rest of us didn't start for another year. They were there to see Karen, not me. I knew that, but it still felt good to have them there and be part of it.

Karen suggested we play a game of strip poker. I was surprised that she would say that, nervous about us sitting in an open garage having a garage sale and taking our clothes off, terrified that Dave and Dan didn't really want to see me with my clothes off. Everyone was looking at me. I said, "Okay."

Smiled to cover up my fear. Scanned in my head to see if I had decent underwear on, if there were any zits on my butt right now. There weren't, I didn't think, but I couldn't remember if I had checked this morning, or if I was just remembering that because I wanted to.

Dan and Dave were cute. Blonde with carved out noses and nice bodies. Although too damn short. Everyone was too damn short for me. And Karen was dark, sun-tanned, with long shiny black walnut hair. I thought she was beautiful. Could never figure out why she was my friend. Me: too tall, hair that Mom had chopped off in a pixie cut last year that still hadn't grown back, no breasts, plain. The three of them were beautiful and popular. And then there was me. All four of us about to play strip poker in Karen's grandmother's open garage with the rain pouring down outside and Karen's grandmother dying on the bed inside.

"Who's going to shuffle and deal?" Karen asked, looking at me.

I didn't want to, wasn't good at it, was nervous already, hadn't ever played cards much. Poker never. Strip poker never times two. My family played Clue and Monopoly.

I said, "I will." And I did. Ineptly, but I got those cards shuffled and dealt.

Karen lost first. She took out the clip that was holding her long hair back. I was hugely relieved. I had two clips, a choker, two earrings, and a ring. Plus shoes, socks, a belt, and a jacket.

Dave said, "Hey, that's cheating. If clips and jewelry count, we're going to be here all day getting you stripped down. You've got twice as much underwear as we do anyway."

Karen just looked at him. "Tough. We didn't agree on any rules before we started, so that's the way it is. You guys'll just have to play a little better than we do if you're not wanting to wind up naked in a garage in the rain."

Dave looked from Karen to Dan and shrugged, "Okay then, we'll just play one whole hell of a lot better. We ain't gonna be the ones naked in a garage in the rain."

They didn't play better. I played the best, won the most times. Which somehow felt like losing. When we heard Karen's grandmother call, Dave and Dan were both sitting in the garage with nothing left on but white cotton underwear just like my little brother's. Sitting in the garage with white cotton underwear all stretched funny around their penises now. Their penises trying to look out at Karen.

Karen had lost two barrettes, her necklace, both earrings, her shoes and socks, her belt, and her shirt. She looked beautiful sitting there shirtless. Lacy white bra, silky black walnut hair framing those gorgeous breasts.

I was somehow embarrassed to be sitting there with all my clothes on. Everything but one shoe. Like they had somehow cheated to make sure I was the one to win.

I said to Karen, did you know that

31

if you touch yourself like this,
a good feeling comes?

I was embarrassed around Karen a lot. She was bright and funny and confident. I was always too tall and too tongue-tied and on the edge of things.

When I was twelve, the summer before the strip poker game at the garage sale, I was over at Karen's house for an outside slumber party and it was late. Dark. The telling-secrets time. The Oreos and Coke were gone, and our stomachs were a little sick from too many too fast.

"Let's play Truth-or-Dare," Karen said.

I said, "Okay. I get to ask first." I didn't want to tell first. Didn't have anything to tell.

"Okay, go," she said.

I thought a minute. "Tell me something secret you've done at night."

Karen said, "I'll tell you if you promise not to tell anyone."

I promised. Cross my heart and cut off my breasts.

She said, "I kissed Dave Erickson at the park on Thursday. Now my turn."

"Wait a minute!" I said, "That's not fair. You have to tell the whole story. That's how it always is."

Karen laughed. "Okay. Just testin' . . . I was walking the back way, down where there are no lights, smoking a cigarette, and Dave came up behind me and grabbed me and pulled me down on to the grass. I screamed when he

32

grabbed me because I didn't know who it was, but then he said, 'It's okay, it's just me,' and I relaxed a little. Almost peed my pants first though. He rolled me over and then laid down on top of me and started kissing me. And then he started feeling my breasts."

I was sitting there with my mouth open looking stupid. "Then what happened?"

"Nothing. That was all. In a minute I told him to get off of me, I was going home, and when he didn't I hit him until he did. Now it's my turn to ask."

I was nervous, didn't have anything to tell her that was like that. "Okay, ask."

"Tell me something secret you've done at night."

Crap. I thought about it for a minute, and then said, "I haven't done anything secret at night."

Karen said, "That's no fair. You have to answer, too."

I thought another minute, then decided to tell her The Secret. The one no one else knew about. I said, "Well, did you know that if you roll over on your stomach like this . . ." I rolled over on my stomach. ". . . and put your hand underneath you like this . . ." I put my hand underneath me. ". . . and then move around on it like this . . ." I moved around on my hand. ". . . that this really good feeling will come if you do it long enough?" I didn't do it long enough.

I rolled back over and laid there for a few minutes, looking up at the stars, waiting for Karen to say something. Karen didn't say anything. I finally looked over and Karen was just looking at me. Looking at me like she couldn't believe I had told her that. Looking at me like maybe I was

33

a total and complete idiot and didn't know the things you aren't supposed to say.

That's what I felt like. A total and complete idiot. I had really thought this would be a gift to her. Something she wouldn't know about. And it felt so good, I wanted her to feel that too. But I had obviously done something wrong. Something horribly wrong and now maybe Karen wouldn't be my friend anymore. I'd been waiting for that for years. For Karen to decide not to be my friend anymore. And now that would probably happen.

Karen and I didn't say anything else to each other that night. I quit looking at Karen and started looking at the stars again. I wished Karen would say something, but she didn't say anything else that night. I didn't go to sleep for a long time.

The next morning, Karen and I seemed to be okay. I knew that what I'd said was something we would never talk about. Something I would never talk to anyone else about. One of the stories I would never tell. Or at least not for a very long time. One of those things that stay with you forever and make you feel embarrassed and like you want to die every time you remember them.

We dance towards truth
cringe
fall back

When we were in eighth grade—the last year that Karen was my best friend—we heard somewhere that you could get high smoking nutmeg. We'd also heard you could get high smoking banana peels, but then we'd heard that wasn't true, so we decided on the nutmeg. We were going to an 'away' game, a high school game, the next night and wanted to get high. Later that year, I bought one half-ounce of pot from Jim Stolz for ten dollars, but for just right then, neither of us had any way of getting any real drugs. So we walked down the hill into town to get some nutmeg. We'd heard it had to be whole nutmeg, that the dried kind wouldn't work. So we got a box of whole nutmegs and then I took two knives from the kitchen, and one afternoon while Mom was still at work, we hid out in the garage to shave the nutmegs.

It took forever. Nutmegs are really hard to shave—at least with steak knives—and Karen and I spent all afternoon in the garage shaving those suckers down, making little piles of nutmeg on coffee cup saucers. We finally decided we had enough. More from being tired of shaving nutmegs than from having enough.

Then we realized we needed something to roll it in, so I went in the house and got some tinfoil and we rolled up two nutmeg-tinfoil joints.

We were very excited to go to the game. It was out at Barlow, and neither of us had ever been there. Her parents were dropping us off, and Mom was letting me go with her alone, which was a minor miracle. The other minor miracle being that it was just Karen and I, no other friends. That I would have her to myself for a whole night.

We watched the first part of the game, but were really just scoping out the landscape. Seeing what guys were there that we might like to meet, looking for a place to go light our nutmeg-tinfoil joints where no teachers or adults could see us. It started raining halfway through the first quarter. At half-time, Karen and I went over to some blackberry bushes on the far side of the field and huddled in behind them. In the pouring rain,we tried to light fresh nutmeg in wet tinfoil. We got it lit just enough, about six times, to get that taste permanently engraved in our taste-buds, but not enough to actually get a hit off it. It tasted like, I don't know what—fresh nutmeg in wet tinfoil.

So our great sinful doping escapade was pretty much a bust. We got that after the sixth time we tried to light it. Even if we could get it to stay lit, we didn't want to get high bad enough to do any serious inhalation of that particular substance.

The good news was that two high school guys came along with a fifth of Black Velvet and rescued us. I don't remember anything else about that night, or those guys, except it was a huge relief that it hadn't been a bust after all.

You two always do this.
No, mama, we don't.

36

Our freshman year in high school, Karen was still my friend. I didn't understand it. Still my best friend. Although I wasn't her best friend any more. Karen had lots of friends that were more 'best' than me by now. Karen was popular and pretty and everyone liked her. Liked her a lot.

She was good at sports, and good at singing, and liked to party. She was funny and happy and she always had boys around her. Asking her out. Being her friend.

But, in spite of all that, Karen was never mean to me. Never ignored me in the hall when I said hi, sometimes would do something with me when I asked, every once in a while would ask me to do something.

One day, pretty close to the beginning of school, Karen asked me if I wanted to go with her and some other kids to smoke pot at lunch. Karen's lunch was the one before mine, but I decided to skip Biology and go anyway. I was really excited to be asked to go do something with her and the other kids she hung around with.

I met Karen at the end of the tennis courts at 11:30 and we walked over together. We walked down to the Chevron station at the end of the block and went around to the back side where no one could see us. It started sprinkling when we were walking over. There were four girls and one guy there—Karen and Janet and Tami and Fred and me. Karen and Janet and Tami were all popular. Fred was sort of popular. He had the pot.

Fred died in a holly field somewhere.

37

Karen lit the joint and we started passing it around. Janet and Tami and I were standing under the eaves where it was all the way dry. Karen and Fred weren't quite covered up, but they leaned in to keep the joint dry when it was their turn.

We had just about finished the joint when, with no warning, a huge amount of water came down on Karen's head. Soaked her, head to toe—great clothes, great hair, perfectly minimal makeup and all. The rest of us just stood there staring. Karen just stood there dripping. None of us said anything for a minute and then Karen looked up and said, "Shit, let's go, there's a guy on the roof with another bucket of water!"

We got back after second lunch had already started and tried to dry Karen off as best we could in the loop of the towel dispenser in the bathroom. Then the bell rang and Karen and I had to go to Mrs. Angdon's class. Mrs. Angdon—the dragon lady of English. Actually, I liked her, but she did scare the shit out of me. And me stoned was pretty easy to scare the shit out of just on general principles.

Mrs. Angdon looked at Karen funny when we walked in the door. Said, "Got caught in the rain, did you Karen?" Gave Karen a look that made me think she knew how Karen got wet, then gave me a look that made me *know* she knew what I had been doing.

I didn't smoke pot at school very often after that.

Karen moved to Ohio that next year.

> *Don't leave.*
> *I like the skyline of my life.*

STILL SATURDAY. . .

I am of the considered opinion that all writers are Schizophrenic Manic Depressives With Paranoid Delusions Of Grandeur.

But then I'm no clinician, so what the hell do I know?

Other than that I know you have to be moderately insane to lock yourself up in a room for three days believing you are going to finish a Novel.

Not that all writers do that, of course.

More of a personal problem, actually.

And that moderate insanity ain't gonna get the sucker finished. You're going to have to go all the way insane to finish.

Not too long a way from here. Should be no problem.

There are piles and piles of paper on the bed, and only thirty pages finished. Thirty pages of complete and total shit. None of it matching the rest, two good paragraphs at last count. Fairly grotesquely out of order.

But, golly gee, what a great Learning Experience this is being! (*Insert slightly twisted simpering sweet smile.*) Fuck me.

There are some things I really don't want to know about myself.

I was in another writing workshop the week before the one I met Mat in. I'm not a workshop junkie, it just happens that the only two I have taken in my life were back-to-back a month ago.

Fifteen women and one man. Tough room. For men in general, that is. Stan actually handled it pretty well. Seemed to be about twelve women in there with that covertly-to-blatantly-vicious feminist sense of humour that insists women are better than men.

I keep feeling like that's somehow missing the point.

We were writing long short stories. Aiming at sixteen pages in the five-day class.

Which reminds me to point out to myself that up until a month ago, I had no stories over eight manuscript pages. Nothing that had not been completed in one sitting. To point out to myself that, as much fun as I am *not* having now, in one month I have busted through the eight-page wall and the one-sitting wall, and that this Novel—shit or not—pretty much disintegrates whatever rubble is left lying around my ankles from that.

> *It was big.*
> *It was fucking big.*

Anyway, in the workshop we'd been working together for four days and were on the final readings of the 'theoretically finished' drafts of our stories. We couldn't read our own stuff, had to listen to someone else read it and then listen to sixteen other people critique it, which was a Useful Exercise, another one of those great Learning Experiences.

The author who was teaching this class had already told me she wasn't sure she was qualified to critique my work. It had too strong a poetic bent—and she didn't read poetry. Had no affinity for it. Couldn't get into it.

Margi asked to read my work. Which made me glad because Margi had come up to me the day before, after I'd been fairly soundly beaten about the head and ears for not coming right out and saying "What I put my foot in was a cobweb" in my story. Said she'd known it was a cobweb, had liked the "something twisted, cloying, sticky and breaking between my toes" imagery I had used. Said she liked my writing because it was different, had a poetic feeling to it.

Well, that story did, anyway.

So Margi read my story. Did a nice job, too. It was a pretty good first draft story—toggled back and forth between an adult relationship with a female main character and a male lover, and a story about a little girl discovering her grandmother's trunk of secrets in the attic.

During the critique part of the readings it always took a while for anyone to say anything negative. Had to get all the sweetness and light out of the way. Judith was sitting across from me. Judith said, "I want to know how the sweet little girl in the attic grew up to be a toilet fucker."

The sweetness and light was out of the way.

Felt like Judith sorta missed the point of the story. Sat

there for a minute with my mouth open, deciding whether to be amused or hurt. Decided on amused. Hid what little hurt was lurking underneath the "She just doesn't get it." "I don't know," I said.

> *Every time I say this out loud it scares me.*
> *Scares me that I should know,*
> *that the other person does,*
> *that I'm stupid,*
> *that someone will go away.*

One scene in one story and the character is automatically defined as a toilet fucker. There seemed to be some consensus on that. Not by everyone, but by the women in the workshop who would never consider fucking on a chair in an unused bathroom in an old warehouse-turned-concert-hall. Every one of them took three paragraphs out of twelve pages as the definition of this character, this relationship. Sleazy, as another of them said. Looked at me different after that.

I suppose the fact that there was even a question about whether I was going to be amused or hurt by Judith's comment is a dead giveaway that there was some basis in reality for the story. I suppose I could say that it was just a writer's natural protectiveness towards her characters. But that would be a fiction, in a fiction.

A friend from next door asked, was this story true? "Parts of it," I said. "Parts of it," I could say to any story I have ever written. Or I could just say, "Yes," because all of what I've written is somehow true. Even if you don't believe the main character. That is a fault only of the writing, not the story.

SUNDAY

Two of us are sitting, writing stories, in my cabin by the river. The cabin is really a guest house. Separated from the main house, where I live in the winter, by a few feet of deck. Surrounded by trees, river just on the other side of the trees. Nice deck outside where I sit and write. Where Mat and I go to eat or have a cigarette. I have planted fuschias and impatiens in green planters all along the top of the deck railings except where I have my view of the river between two trees.

It is cold in the winter to go out to the guest house, but just yet it is not winter. It is still summer, though the tail end of summer, so we sit in sweatshirts and jeans in the not-quite-chill of a rainy afternoon.

The birds outside have been noisy today. The jays coming by regularly looking for food, screeching when there is none to be found, the kingfishers and herons scrawing by on the river, the ospreys overhead crying their hunting cries. The chipmunk has been to the feeder regularly. I notice some kind of grass growing thick between the fuschia and impatiens in the planter below. Some kind of grass that was once some seed the chipmunk and jays, I figured, didn't like.

Mat and I wrote for hours today. Got up at seven, wrote until three. Some of it flowed, some of it stuck. Lots of cigarette breaks. I stood up at three to take a shower, and when I sat down again, there was nothing there. No words, no body, no voice to ask for help. No direction, no use of eyes for anything but tears. I left for four hours. I'm still not back. Am writing blinded. Am writing unable to feel the words moving up through my body. Am writing with no direction towards story or message or even the next event. Just writing. Because that is what I wish to do. Because I do truly want badly to complete this. Because, at base, a writer is what I am. Part of what I am.

I am pushing the edge of something old here, something that runs deep hard long to push me that far out without warning. I don't know what it is, have no choice now but to write down to it or get stuck in it. Since writing is what I am doing, writing is what I will do. You're along for the ride. Like it or not.

Most live.
Hopefully not just to be squashed
two hours later.

I have resisted writing a story about me writing a story.

Have always believed that one of the things that marks a good story is the inability for the reader to "see" the writer writing. I still believe that. But just right now this once that is not an option I have been given. So be it.

I can't see. I can't speak. I can't feel.
I have lost my sight, lost my voice,
lost my body somewhere in the
place between. I don't know how to get back.
Even to me. Even to the words that are mine.
I am sitting here in the blind dark quiet
isolation
unable to touch anything,
unable to be touched.
and all is vacant dark disconnected
here in the place between.

Mat is here with me today. And yesterday. And tomorrow. Locked up in a small room with three dogs in a cabin by the river. She is good. As a writer. As a friend. As someone to be there when things are hard. When the hurt came, and the tears, she let me be for what seemed like a long time. Once she turned around and said, "So, how's it goin'?"

I said, "It's a little rocky, right now." She smiled and turned back around. And then I cried some more, and wrote a screaming prayer in my writing book, and cried again, and after a while she came to a break in her story and went to pee. And while she was in the bathroom I pulled myself together enough to know that I was not making it any easier for her to write. I looked at her when she came back in and said, "Hi there." She looked steady deep in my eyes and said, "How are you doing?"

And, crying again, I said, "Well, I can't see, I can't speak, and I am totally disconnected. Other than that, everything's peachy."

She asked, "Is there anything I can do?"

Which made the tears start harder, which made me not able to look at her. I said, "No, I don't think so." Wanting to ask for something. Not knowing what it was I could ask for that would be *okay* for me to ask for.

She said, "Do you want a hug?" And I said, "If you touch me, I will go right over the edge."

Wanting more than anything to be touched, to be pushed over the edge so I wouldn't have to stay here teetering on the brink any longer. But that's not what I said. What I said sounded like *no*. So she honoured that and went outside to handroll a Drum. She pulled the chair away from the table by the door and, as I saw the chair, saw her, moving further away, my heart screamed NO, don't move way from me, I need you to move closer, I need you to not listen to my words, I need you here. And I am afraid. Always afraid right in this spot, this spot where I have no words, where I feel unprotected and easily hurt. The only thing in this place that I know how to do is hide. Go down into it and hide. Please don't move away from me while I am here in this place.

I have been reading Grandma's stories this week. The ones she put together in a hardbound black book and sent out to all the family two years before she died. I didn't read them then. Didn't read them until this last week.

These are Grandma's stories. Some of Grandma's stories. Because just right now from this place I am hiding in I can't tell you my stories.

And because Grandma's stories are mine. I can feel her stories in me, my stories in her.

GRANDMA, MAY 27, 1987 . . .

I am getting old. Am feeling almost ready to die. I wake most mornings hurting everywhere, my hands do not work as well as they once did, my legs will only support me for short periods of time. I am tired down to the bone.

I am feeling not at all ready to die. Too many stories still to tell. Things I need to finish before I am ready to release this body. I must keep writing down these stories of what is in me to tell you.

I have perhaps told too many stories already in my life. Certainly I have told some stories too many times, but yet somehow it seems that I have left much unsaid. Or poorly said. I don't wish to die without my story being told. Without telling my story once with at least a little grace.

I don't know that grace is in me. Certainly there are many of my friends, many of my family, who would say it is not. And yet I think that perhaps it is here in me, that perhaps I have just somehow not been able to show it well.

That perhaps my grace has not fully been seen by all those many people I have loved. Or, more truly, that I have hidden it for these almost eighty years.

GRANDMA, JULY 3, 1987 . . .

My name is Moira. Born Thomas. I was born when this newest century was just ten, trying to find its feet. Just beginning to know what it was. I was born in Platte, South Dakota, the youngest then of five children. Born when there was already not enough to go around. Born when another girl was not a full blessing. Three older brothers, one older sister, later one younger. Ruth was the oldest— always angry with me, always bossing, always wanting things to go all her way. And most of the time they did. Beth was born a year and a half after me, my playmate and confidante through all the growing up times. Beth and I didn't lose each other until later.

My brothers were William, Carl and Lane—wild when they were young, never settled into growing up. Which is understandable, neither did their father—my father: cop, postman, gambler, bootlegger, adulterer, ne'er-do-well— his only rule for the boys was, don't get caught. William got caught. He was killed in World War I in France the day after Armistice. He was much older than me, although I caught up fast when he died. William got caught before I was old enough to know much about him. I only remember two things about him. One, a Thanksgiving dinner in Platte. I was probably about four, still sitting on the big family Bible to get my chin up over the table. William leaned his chair back on two legs after he'd finished his third helping of chicken, folded his hands on his belly, let out a wail loud enough to start the dogs barking outside while his chair went backwards in slow motion. He hit the hardwood floor with a sound like breaking. His head started bleeding out the back and his eyes wouldn't open. William was dead in the war before I found out he had screamed because his appendix had burst when he tipped his chair back. I never in my life have tipped my chair back on two legs.

The second memory I have of William is of him throwing me in the air and catching me, throwing me and catching me, throwing me up in the air and always catching me.

My mother and father had some sort of agreement about us kids, and that's always how it was. Dad was in charge of the boys, teaching them to not get caught, but Mother had different rules for the girls. Substantially different rules. Our rules were strict, really strict, but Mother probably felt she had to be strict with our rules, given who my Dad was and how wild the boys were getting. I didn't feel like it then, but now I'm glad she was strict, because her strictness kept us girls more or less on the straight and narrow.

When I was about five, Dad was a policeman. Actually, Platte was so small that Dad was *the* policeman. It was the second-to-last respectable job he ever had. We lived above a restaurant then, a restaurant that Mother operated without any help from Dad. Mother was tired a lot then, hands full of kids and doing everything to keep the house going and the restaurant. Cooking and cleaning and serving, not just for our family, but for a whole town, even if Platte wasn't very big.

Mother was beautiful. Tall for the time, and dark, with deep calm eyes you could fall right into. And always gentle with us. I sometimes wonder how I turned out to be so ornery. Maybe one of us had to.

Those were hard times for everyone, but seemed especially hard for the women. There was little money, many lived in isolation, families were big, and the work was grueling. Women went insane a lot. Or what we deemed insane at the time, which was often what we would now probably call a nervous breakdown, or simple exhaustion. When a man would go insane, he was held in the jail until he could be transported to State; but Platte was so small that there were no facilities for holding the women, so Mom, as the wife of the only policeman in town, was responsible for keeping those women at the house until it was time for them to go. During the days, they would have to be kept in the restaurant where Mom could keep an eye on them. At night, they would be handcuffed to the bed in the extra room where guests would stay.

Sometimes love feels like such an
incredible violence.

Merilee Pond went truly insane one spring. She was certain that her husband was cheating on her after she went to

52

sleep at night. So she tied a silver thread between two corn-stalks outside their bedroom window figuring that he would break it, unseeing, if he snuck out to see his mistress while Merilee was asleep.

A wind came up, as it did most nights, the cornstalks moved in the wind, swayed back and forth. The thread broke.

When Merilee woke up, her husband was lying still asleep next to her and she went out to find the silver thread hanging broken between two stalks of corn. Merilee in her white flannel nightgown took the hatchet off the woodpile, went back into the house, and hacked her husband to death in his sleep.

Which is how she got to our house. We kids were a lit-tle afraid of her, although she seemed quiet enough, nice enough. She had been with us two days and we hadn't seen her cry, or yell, or do anything we could see as being crazy. She just sat quietly handcuffed to a chair in the restaurant during the day, slept quietly handcuffed to her bed at night. By the start of the third day, we got bold. Went over to where Merilee was sitting in the restaurant, Beth and I did, and sat down near enough to her to talk. Far enough away that she couldn't reach out and strangle us between her handcuffed hands. Beth was scared, so I did the talking.

"Excuse me, Miz Pond," I said. "Would you like us to talk with you for a little while?"

Merilee Pond smiled. She had a pretty smile, pretty face. "Yes," she said, "I would like that very much. You're Moira and Beth, aren't you?"

"Yes, ma'am," I said. "Aren't you uncomfortable with your hands like that?"

"Yes, Moira, I am. But you know I killed my husband with these hands, so I guess people feel like these hands need to be tied up to keep people safe." Merilee Pond was looking at me deep. Like she could see everything about me that I'd always kept hidden. All the bad things. It scared me a little, but it felt good, too.

I said, "But you would never hurt anyone else, would you Miz Pond?"

She thought for a minute, like she never expected anyone to ask her that question. Like she had never asked herself that question. Then she said, sort of surprised sounding, "Why no, Moira, I surely wouldn't."

Merilee Pond and I talked for a while longer, with Beth sitting there with her eyes all wide. We talked just about things. About me helping at the restaurant, and about the horse getting hurt on the fence, about Merilee when she was young and met her husband and fell in love. Merilee asked me to call her Merilee, instead of Miz Pond. Merilee said she would like to be my friend, that she felt like she needed a friend right now. I told her I wasn't quite six yet, and Merilee said she had been looking for a friend of just that age.

That third morning Merilee was with us, the morning Merilee asked me to be her friend, the restaurant was busy for breakfast. Mother was working hard taking orders, cooking eggs, and serving coffee. So when Merilee told Mother she had to go to the bathroom, Mother asked me to escort Merilee to the outside privy.

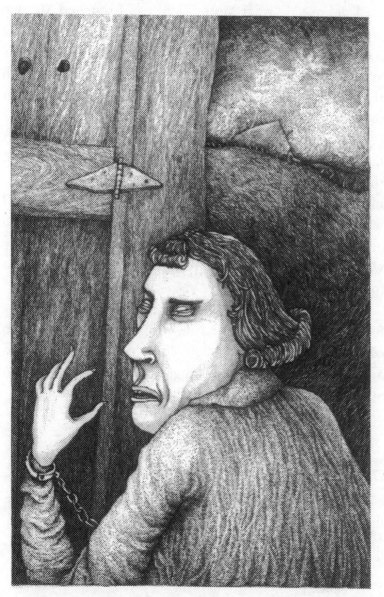

Merilee was gone . . . and was nowhere to be found.

I did exactly what Mother told me. I watched Merilee go into the privy, I stood with my back against the door and waited. And waited. And waited. It seemed like I waited a very long time for her to come back out. I was going to call through the door to see if she was okay, but I didn't want to be rude.

Just when I was starting to get scared that Merilee was maybe hurt or sick in there, Mother came rushing out of the restaurant to see what was going on. She told me to move out of the way, to go stand over by the apple tree, and when Mother opened the door of the privy, there was no one inside. Merilee was gone. She had crawled out the tiny window in the back of the privy and was nowhere to be found.

The men searched for Merilee for three days. They found her curled in a little ball, covered with straw, in the corner of the Smith's hayloft down the road about two miles. Merilee was never brought back to our house. No one in Platte ever saw her again.

I never saw her again.

GRANDMA, SEPTEMBER. 22, 1987 . . .

I have no words today. Too many words to begin to write them.

> *It is so hard at times*
> *to know what it is I need to say*
> *what it is I must remember*

to know I have not much time,
not nearly enough
to tell all that I would.
Which are the stories that
rise from my centre,
that live in my core?

GRANDMA, JANUARY 14, 1988 . . .

Fifty-five years Hal and I were together. Married in 1930, when both of us were twenty. Hal just five months older than me.

Oh beloved husband, you,
yes, you, are a story
that lives in my core.
So long together,
wait one little while longer
for me to come back to you.
I will come. I will come. Soon.

I wanted a walk-in closet upstairs. Had wanted one for years but somehow it seemed to never quite get to the top of the list with Hal working so hard. We hadn't started world traveling yet, but Hal was out of town a lot, and the boys were both out of the house now, with families of their own. He was making good money and I hadn't had to hold a job for years. So maybe time was a little heavy on my hands.

But, mostly, I just wanted that walk-in closet.

Hal walked out the door to go down to Portland for a week to do some required training to keep his engineer's license current. As soon as I heard the car pull out of the driveway I ran downstairs to the basement, grabbed the saw, and headed upstairs to make a closet. I had been sawing for about twenty minutes and had a nice-sized hole in the wall, about the time I heard our car pull back into the driveway. I dusted off my hands and my front and ran back down the stairs, sat down fast at the dining room table and started working the crossword leftovers from breakfast. Broke all known stair-speed records. Was panting only a little when Hal walked in. Looked up casually.

"Well, hi, honey. Forget something?"

He laughed. "Nothing important, just my briefcase."

Then he took another look at me and said, "What's going on?"

Well, as Hal always said, I'd never lie to him. But I'd sure run around and around and once again around the bend before I got to the truth. So I did a couple laps and then told him. His eyes got really wide fast and he said, "Oh my God, you haven't cut through any structural supports, have you?"

He was already halfway up the stairs before I could open my mouth to answer. Structural supports? What did I know from structural supports? I was just cutting a hole for a walk-in closet in a wall.

By the time I got to the top of the stairs, he was sitting on the bed staring at the hole in the wall. At the mess of plaster and blue-flowered wallpaper and hunks of wall all over the carpet. Then at me standing in the doorway wondering what all the fuss was about. His mouth quirked a little at the edges, and when he looked back at the hole where the wall used to be, he started to laugh. Laughed so hard and so long I thought he would throw up. Until finally he choked out, "Good God, woman, don't ever take on another home improvement project when I'm not around. You'll bring the whole damned house down around our ears."

Hal framed in the hole I'd made when he got back from Portland. Hung a rod. Got me my walk-in closet.

I always told Hal that I could do a project wrong three times while he was still planning how to do it right once. I often did.

Oh what a sweetness you are still to me,
even three years gone.
Your calm to my anger,
your order to my chaos,
your love to my love.

GRANDMA, MARCH 10, 1988 . . .

We had to leave Platte when the restaurant burned down. When I was just past six years old. We were going to visit Mother's parents—on our first train trip—the next week, and Mother had reminded Dad that while we were gone, to pay the insurance on the restaurant and our place above the restaurant right away. Dad promised to remember. No way would he forget that, that's what he said.

But that promise was as good as every other promise he made to Mother, and when the restaurant burned to the ground the next week, we had nothing left but the clothes on our backs and in our suitcases. Between losing everything fast like that, and six kids, we never got on our feet again.

Dad decided it was time to leave Platte, and got us two covered wagons to make the move to Faith, South Dakota. I never knew why he picked Faith as the next place we were going to live, but we loaded up what little we had left in the world and headed out the track towards Faith.

We moved into a sod house with comics for wallpaper. The walls were eighteen inches thick, which made great places in the windows to curl up and watch outside or read or write or play with our dolls or just think. The whole house was papered inside with newspapers, mostly funnies. And Beth and I used to spend hours contorting our bodies into weird positions to be able to read those strips. It was like a magic house to the two of us. Made special just for us.

The day we arrived in Faith at the sod house, the people who lived there before us were auctioning off all their belongings in the hardpack dirt front yard. That family was just the husband and the wife and one small boy. They were selling everything because the wife had gone mad and had to be put into an asylum. It seemed like a lot of women went mad then. It used to scare me when I was little that I would grow up and go mad.

We never found out exactly what had happened, but I heard later that there used to be two boys in that family and I wondered. I wondered if she had gone mad and killed the other one, or if the other one had been killed and she had gone mad. But it could have been something else entirely. That's just what I wondered then.

Every time the auctioneer hollered "Sold!" and pointed his gavel at someone in the crowd, the wife would scream like a cat with its tail slammed in the pantry door, and tear at her hair. I could see clumps of long black hair in her fists each time the auctioneer pointed his gavel.

And she seemed somehow almost the sanest one of the bunch. Her husband and the little boy were so sad, so beaten, that it didn't seem they had any life left to them at all. They were more like shadows, or ghosts, of her. It made me a little afraid of that sod house with the funny papers on the wall.

But I loved that house. Loved living there with the funnies, and later the horses and the bunnies, and a couple years later, the school where I had other kids to play with.

It was not as good a time for Mom. Truth was, Dad was not the kind of man you would choose for a husband. He started in Faith with a job as a mail carrier, but branched out fairly soon into gambling and bootlegging. And, always, he had other women on the side. Dad got his first car in Faith, to cover his mail route, and it apparently enhanced either his image with the women or his lack of discretion in seeing them. When I was seven he brought a teenage girl home with him in that Model T with the side curtains. Mother raised her voice. Impressively. Mother asked the girl to leave with no room for discussion; but nothing like the way she asked my Dad to take the girl home. I really don't believe, and don't think Mother did either, that poor girl was expecting to walk into a house with a wife and six children at home. Dad, however, clearly was aware he had a wife and six children and got no such amnesty. It was the first time I ever heard Mother raise her voice, and it was terrifying. All of us kids left the house, glad that it wasn't us she was mad at.

The other main incident of Dad fooling around, of Mother standing up to Dad fooling around, that I remember was when Mother told us to get dressed up and go visiting for the afternoon. We were going to the house of a divorcée who worked in our restaurant to play with her two girls. We were dumbfounded and thrilled. Mother never allowed us to go to anyone's home to visit. Not alone.

We had a great afternoon playing with the two girls. The mother stayed near us and kept looking out the window. She ran out the front door, and one of the girls said, "Your Dad's here." Beth and I jumped up, thinking he had come to pick us up, but one of the girls said, "Oh, he'll come in. He always does."

Dad didn't come in. He drove away fast.

Dad asked Mother for a divorce that night. We weren't

trying to listen, but we could hear everything through those walls, and they were talking pretty loud. My mother said, "No, there will be no divorce. I will never permit a divorce so you can start another family to neglect as you have this one."

Dad yelled a bunch of stuff I can't really remember. But I remember Mother saying calmly back to him, "Do you even know how many times you've asked for a divorce to marry some other woman? Well, I do. This is the sixth time. And the answer is still no." That was the end of the argument, although Dad's yelling went on for some time into the night.

The divorcée quit work and left town the next day.

GRANDMA, MAY 5, 1988 . . .

It is hard right now to keep writing. My hands are hurting me, too many stories are crowding in to be heard and yet, somehow, none of them feel to be the essence of the thing. Life is precious and limited, and I feel a mistake made now, a wrong choice, will find me at the end of my time with the one crucial thing I have to say left unsaid.

> *I have not learned in my life*
> *to ration my world into time,*
> *have most often followed*
> *what was there in the moment,*

doing what I most wanted,
and now still I find there is something
something . . .

It felt once like I had all the time in the world.

STILL SUNDAY, NIGHT NOW

Mat said she'd give me ten bucks if I could use all the slips on the wall, on the ceiling, in my story.

I said, "Only ten bucks?"

She said, "That's all I've got."

Oh.

This has been a hard day. It feels like not even the same day as the one we started this morning. Feels like there have been many days in this day of writing for fifteen hours.

We are not being very kind to our bodies. Smoking too much, eating crap, not sleeping to renew what we have used in the course of the day. We did take the dogs for a walk. Wore them out. We already were.

Mat and I looked at each other tonight, both exhausted. All systems tapped.

I said, "What the fuck are we doing?"

Mat said, "You know, we don't have to do this. We could get up in the morning and decide to go sit in the hot tub and then come back and throw these files in the garbage. Or just let go of the deadline."

I said, "We could do that."

Sleep now.

Real time—now time—the moving forward from Saturday where we started, to now, which is Sunday, to now, which is Monday, is a bit difficult to deal with in this sucker. Normally I would be writing from a static position. Looking back on something that happened before, or moving forward consistent with some logical progression. This now being Saturday, and this now being Sunday seems like a fairly logical progression, but somehow it's not working. So since I don't have ten years to puzzle through the problem, I'm simply going to say . . .

It's Monday.

MONDAY

The first cigarette of the day usually makes me feel like shit. Except for the days when it's been a long time since the last cigarette of the day before. Days when I've slept a long time. Today isn't one of those.

But on those days it's a pretty decent legal head rush. Gives me that swirly feeling. Sort of the same as the swirly feeling of smoking pot, or great sex, or in that half-dreaming place on the edge of sleep. I love that swirly feeling. Love it best when it comes from sex or dreaming. Doesn't last long enough with a cigarette and I don't much smoke pot anymore.

He said, it's sort of like eating
a fat-free Twinkie—
you just don't do that.

My sometimes-lover called this morning at six-thirty. No one calls me at six-thirty. Called to see if he could break the flow of the writing by talking dirty to me. Has sort of a perverse playfulness at times.

Mat groaned from her red, scotty-dog-covered cocoon when the phone rang. So I wrapped the kimono more or less around me and went out on the deck. Was out there for an hour. Feet got a little chilly. Didn't seem to hurt the writing a bit. May sign up for calls on a regular schedule.

I turn on the computer. Look at BODYWORD.DOC. Don't want to open it.

Note that OUTOMIND.DOC and TRYAGAIN.DOC are still sitting there leering at me. Refuse to open them.

I open a new file. Call it BODYFUCK.DOC.

We have apparently decided to keep writing. Sleep helped.

Not taking this whole thing so damn seriously, being willing to walk away, probably helped more.

You know who it is, don't you?
Yes.
You're going to kill them, aren't you?
Yes.

Mat is typing away across the room, somewhat less fluently than yesterday. Halting and starting and stretching and belching. The belching part is probably more that both our body systems shut down completely last night and that the

68

vegetarian chili with real hamburger-like chunks of authentic processed vegetable protein is still sitting in our stomachs fourteen hours later. Probably more that than a specific body response to the writing process. Maybe not.

Mat and I have been laughing all morning, telling stories, slightly hysterical edge to the laughter, breaking frequently to smoke and tell another story. Writing some. One whole shitload of a long way to go before midnight rolls around one last time. One last time for this particular process at any rate.

The first sentence of the day:

There are some things that just seem to stick with you forever. Men with hairy backs for one.

I mentioned that to Mat, and we started telling hairy back stories . . .

MY STORY:

My sister lived with me in the house on Ladd Circle, the house where the guy who was sponging off me and fucking me at the time, the guy I found out later was a mafia drug dealer, raped my best friend.

My sister was going out with a guy from the photofinishing plant we both worked in. Since the process of finishing photos involves a bunch of mostly young, universally underpaid, occasionally drugged people working all night long, the social life of people finishing photos tends to consist of other people involved in finishing photos.

There were six marriages out of that plant—that I can think of—in the time I was there. Including mine. Including my sister's.

My sister was going out with a guy from the photofinishing plant we both worked in. This was Mike, and by some polls—yes, we did take polls, informal ones—thought to be the best looking guy in the place. Sun-blond long hair, dark tanned skin on a squarish well-worked body, a good easy smile and big doe-brown eyes that looked right through yours until they seemed to see right into your sex. They looked great together—my sister with her mid-back length sunshiny red-blonde hair and light perfect untannable skin; her pretty face, flat stomach, nice breasts. The Blond River God and Blonde Forest Goddess.

We were out in the front yard of the green house on Ladd Circle one summer afternoon, me supposedly taking a break from all the hard work I'd done on the yard—actually just lying in the sun after doing not a damned thing—and Mike and my sister coming down to help from a late morning sleeping in. Mike offered to mow which, given that it was July, and given that the grass had been growing since late February, and given that the grass had not been mowed once since it started growing, was no small offer.

Everything was going great until Mike took off his shirt. Actually, it kept going great for a couple minutes after Mike took off his shirt. Mike had a great chest. Broad. Nice definition. Good crop of straight long soft blond-brown on his tan. Kept going great until Mike turned the lawnmower around to go in the away-from-me direction.

Mike was a fucking ape. Had the same straight soft

blond-brown hair on his tan back. All the way down his back to the top of his shorts. The same but longer. It was gross. I rolled over on my belly so I didn't have to watch Mike's back mowing my lawn.

I asked my sister how she could stand sleeping with that. I meant fucking that, but I didn't say that as much then. My sister said she liked it, sort of like being in bed with—she meant being in bed with, my sister still doesn't say "fucking" much—a big soft bear. Said it felt good under her fingers, felt good to pet.

I don't particularly want a pet fucking me. Been there, done that. (But that's another story. Which I probably won't tell you later.) Difference in taste, I s'pose.

It's like my Dad always used to say . . . where would we be if we all liked the same things—we'd pretty quick run out of the things we all liked.

I don't think my Dad ever said that exactly, but I'll bet somebody's Dad did.

MAT'S STORY:

There was this guy I liked in high school. Liked him a lot. His name was Derek Darwin. Blond hair, a little higher on the top, great body, dressed mostly in black leather with assorted piercings and danglies. A punk. Older—a senior. Just my type.

Well, I never got close to this guy in weeks and weeks of haunting him. These days what I was doing would be called 'stalking'. Following him around with a camera, always just out of sight, collecting shots to put on the wall over my bed. Pictures of Derek Darwin in between Mick Jagger and David Bowie. Good long nights, those fall-into-winter nights are.

So by January I had pretty much given up on getting Derek any closer to my pelvic fire—as we jokingly called our sweet young cunts in those days. Not that I had done much other than stalk him to get his attention. Nothing much other than that. Nothing much other than telling all my friends I wanted to fuck Derek Darwin, assuming that this bit of information—like everything else secret I had ever told them—would get directly back to the ears which could create the most perceived embarrassment. Nothing much other than arranging my schedule so that I was planted directly in his path at least three times a day between classes. Nothing much other than that. No small wonder we hadn't gotten together yet.

Then came the night of the party. Not that it was The Party—I was partying quite a lot at that time, and there were any number of parties in any given month—but it was the night of the particular party in question.

I had gone to the party with Lisa and Red, and after we'd been there a couple hours and were pretty fucked up, Red came over. She screamed in my ear, "Guess what!"

"Jeezus, tone it down a notch, Red. The fucking music stopped three minutes ago." I rubbed at a spot inside my ear where Red's soundwaves must've bruised my eardrum.

Red lowered her voice half a click, "Oh, sorry. But guess what?" She was clearly over-excited. Or over-medicated. Or both.

I raised my voice slightly. Popped my eyebrows up to indicate eager anticipation of joyous news, and pumped my lungs twice fast so I could say, sweet-like and with the aforementioned eager anticipation, "What, Red, what? Please please tell me!"

Red was apparently not quite as medicated as I had believed. She shot me a look that said, die, bitch, and said, "Eat shit and die, you smartass bitch, I just won't tell you then."

I lowered my voice. Lowered my eyebrows back to their resting position and pulled them slightly in toward the centre of my forehead to indicate contrite concern and said, "I'm sorry, Red. What?"

Red was exactly as medicated as I had believed. She bought. Red lowered her voice another half-click, now that the music had started blasting again, leaned into my ear, and said something I couldn't understand.

I raised my voice three clicks and shouted, "Red! I can't hear you!" and gesticulated wildly in the general direction of the dozen or so bodies thrashing around on the dance floor.

Red looked at the dance floor. Looked back at me. Red had a fairly absent look on her pretty freckled face.

Then she got it. Red screamed, "Oh! Sorry! I said Derek Darwin is here. Outside by the pool!"

Well. No shit.

Felt like it was just about time for a refreshing dip in the pool to me. All sweaty from all this not-dancing, you know. I headed outside, stripped off my shirt on the way, stepped out of my jeans when I got to the edge, dove in

73

right next to a group of guys standing in a tight clutch passing a joint around. Hopefully Derek was somewhere in the middle of that clutch.

I came up on the other end of the pool gasping—discreetly, I hoped—for air. There was a lot of whooping and hollering going on down at the clutch end. Someone yelled, "Hey, Mat! Nice tits!"

I levered my ass up onto the edge of the pool with my nice tits in full view. Offered a tastefully brazen full frontal of the external region of my pelvic fire. Froze my ass to the concrete. Handled it. Yelled back, "Hey thanks, asshole! Why the hell am I the only one in the fucking pool?"

Someone else yelled, "Cuz you're the only one here out of their mind. It's fucking January!"

My turn. "Bunch of no-dick pussies! The pool is heated, dickhead!" Speaking of which, it was past time to get my ass back in that fucking heated pool before I left most of my ass-skin frozen to the side. I slid back in, ducked under, and had gone three long strokes back toward the centre when I felt someone brush underneath me, slide over my tits and my pussy, come up between my legs. I almost choked before I got back up to air. Got back up ready to kill.

Sputtered the water out of my lungs, threw the hair back out of my eyes, looked around for a victim.

Derek was right in front of me. Swimming in his clothes. I couldn't help it, I started laughing. "You're in your fucking clothes, man. Are you out of your mind?"

Derek grinned. Great grin. Reached out and drew a finger from my throat down between my breasts. Stopped at my belly button. "Nah. Just saw an opportunity I wasn't about to let go by and jumped at it. Or in it. Or under it. As the case may be. I'm like that. Spontaneous and carefree, y'know."

I grinned back. Choked on the one last mouthful of water left in my lungs. Said, "Well, you may be spontaneous and carefree, but you're also soon to be one soaked and frozen dickhead when you get out of this pool."

"Frozen dicks are called popsicles, Mat. They're considered a real treat by some." Derek's voice had slipped down a couple of notches and I couldn't hear anything else going on in the world. He grinned again. Great grin. "Wanna come back to my house and try some?"

YES! Down and score!

I usually don't think much in football terms, but this was a special occasion.

"Only if it'll get me out of this fucking pool," I said.

Derek borrowed some clothes from somewhere and we were out of there in ten minutes. Fondling each other in the car in twelve. Back at his house in fifteen. Undressed in eighteen. He had a beautiful cock. Big and hard and with just a little curve up toward his belly. Would've had it in my mouth before we hit nineteen, but just then he turned around to pull the blanket down on the bed.

His fucking back was covered with hair all the way down to his asshole. My pussy froze. My tits went soft. My stomach started churning through chips and pot and beer and tobacco like it just remembered they were in there. When Derek turned back toward me I couldn't even see his fucking dick. Could only see his goddamn baboon back.

75

Tried to see his face, his dick, tried to remember that feeling in my cunt when he brushed underneath me in the pool, scanned for sexy reasons to ask him to put his shirt back on and fuck me that way. But nothing worked, he still had a hairy back. My pussy was still frozen. My tits were still soft.

"Uh, Derek," I said. "Uh, I've been thinking, and, well, uh, I don't think we should do this right now."

Derek looked at me. Looked at me ready to kill me for just a minute. But then his '80s training took over and he said, pretty gently, "Oh? Why is that, Mat?"

"Well," I said, "we don't really know each other. Haven't even ever talked before. It just seems kind of fast."

Derek was still looking at me. Still standing there with his erect dick and his hairy back. He smiled a little. Nice smile. Even under adverse conditions. Said, "That's odd, I'd heard you wanted to fuck me, not talk to me."

Fuck. Fucking cunts did tell him. Fucking asshole knew I wanted to fuck him and still didn't talk to me before. Let's see you pull cool out of this one, bitch.

I looked back at Derek. Shoved the picture of Derek's back away into the back of my brain. Said, "Yeah, that's true. It's just too fast, that's all."

Derek looked at me for a long time. In and out ready to kill me. Got over it. Said, "Okay, cool. Let me get dressed and I'll get you home. Maybe we can do something some-time."

We got dressed. I went home.

Somewhere in there, Derek decided he was in love

with me. Or at least wanted some sort of not-just-fucking relationship with me. Started having flowers sent to me at school. Black flowers. In class. Started calling my house and asking me out several times a week. Showed up at the front door one night wanting to talk to me in person and damn near black-leather-scared my mother to fucking death. She turned out to like him, though. He played the mom thing real good.

Nice guy. No, really—nice guy. Just had this fucking hairy back I couldn't get past.

Derek and I eventually became sorta-friends. He kept popping up at sporadic intervals in my life. One time, much past the night in the swimming pool, when Derek Darwin had popped back into my life for a short while and we were talking, I told him finally about my challenge with his hairy back and he told me this story.

"When I was little, from about three until I was about seven, I wouldn't wear a shirt outside. Not even in the winter. My Mom yelled at me, hit me, forced me to put one on, explained to me why I needed one, did everything she knew to get me to wear a shirt outside when it was cold. I just wouldn't. My body had to grow hair to keep me protected from the cold. That's why my back is so hairy."

Sounded to me like the "How The Elephant Got His Trunk" story. You know, that bad baby elephant who was always getting into things and being made fun of by all the other grownup elephants, until the day he stuck his stubby nose—that all elephants had then—into a pond and the crocodile grabbed on to it and pulled, and pulled, and pulled, and the grownup elephants pulled and pulled and pulled on the other end of the poor baby elephant, and his poor nose stretched, and stretched, and stretched. Until when the crocodile finally let go, the littlest elephant had a great long trunk, as do all elephants ever since.

I don't know quite what to do with the part of the story where the baby elephant goes back and spanks all the grownup elephants with his brand new long trunk for making fun of him. Don't think it has much to do with this story.

Point As It Seems To Be: that Derek Darwin's hairy back being an evolutionary completion of three years of not wearing a shirt pretty much upsets all pre-existing theories of evolution on the books. Think about it.

MAT'S SECOND HAIRY BACK STORY:

I was working for my dad one summer in his lumber company up on the Sound. A couple years into college—Classic Lit—and somewhere past that point when I decided to never again get all dressed up like a girl just to impress the men.

So I was working at my dad's lumber company, wearing scrungy jeans and a white T-shirt—pitted out from manual labouring all day—and a black baseball cap. Makeup wasn't even a possibility. Hadn't been for years. But I looked damn good in that black baseball cap. It always surprised me.

I was working on the second level of the lumber yard warehouse, throwing boxes of nails and screws and other small objects which get fucking heavy en masse down on to the trucks, looking about as female and attractive as Betty Friedan on a bad day, when a new truck pulled in and disgorged a man of about my age I'd never seen before.

I heard a low male whistle from below, then, "Hey, up there! You are one beautiful woman . . . when're you going to let me take you out?"

The man was either sick, blind, or crazy. I hollered back down, "Fucking never, I believe! Thanks for asking so *genteelly*!"

The crazy man hollered back, "Aww, come on. You're the best thing these eyes have seen in a month of Sundays."

Uh huh. I tossed another box of three inch wood screws in his general direction. "Thanks. I guess. I'm not going out with you."

The guy did look highly disappointed. No accounting for taste, I suppose. I mean, unless this guy had x-ray eyes, my current get-up was not my best look. Except for the black baseball cap. He said, "Well, shit. All right then, I'll catch you later."

Bright, too. Takes a hint well. Doesn't let blatant rejection get him down for too long.

Five minutes later the phone rang. Tom called from across the room, "Hey, Mat! Phone!"

It was him.

"Hey, Mat! It's me, the jerk from downstairs. Name's Edgar."

Excuse me? "Edgar?"

Edgar laughed. "Uh, yeah. Dad was a bit eccentric. Means 'wealthy spearman'. Sort of a dumb name for a guy that works with logs, huh?"

I tried not to laugh. This guy didn't need any more encouragement than he came with. "Well, excuse me, Edgar, this may be a dumb question, but why haven't you shortened it to Ed?"

There was silence on the other end of the phone except for the sound of the gears in Edgar's brain whirling away. After a longish pause, during which I considered taking back the question before the systems fouled, the mechanism in his brain engaged with hinges on his jaw, and Edgar said, "I guess I sorta like it."

"Oh."

The longish pause had spread its insidious tentacles to both ends of the phone wire now. Finally, I said, "So, Edgar, not to be more rude than necessary, but I need to get back to work. Did you want something?"

Edgar said, "Yeah, sorry about that, just started thinking about why I'd never shortened my name to Ed, like you said. Got carried away. I just wanted to ask more formally if you would go out with me."

"So was that it?"

Edgar sounded confused. "Was what what?"

This was going to take some time. I breathed deeply from my gut and said, "Was that you asking me more formally to go out with you?"

"Oh," Edgar said, "yeah, that was the formal invitation. Dinner and a movie?"

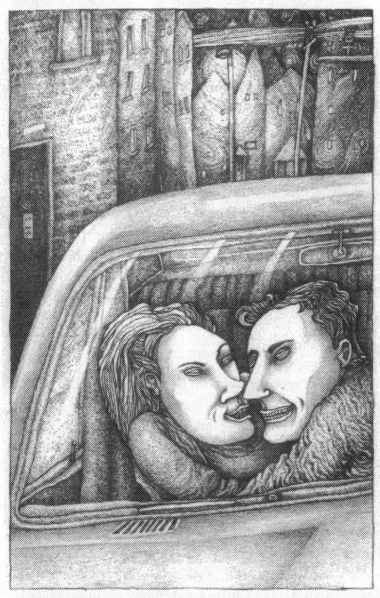

This guy had a couple of endearing qualities. Could be trouble.

I was waffling. Couldn't believe it, but I was waffling.

"Man, Edgar, I don't know. I don't even know anything about you. Other than 'wealthy spearman'."

Edgar laughed. "Actually, you don't know anything about me. I'm not wealthy and I sure ain't no spearman. Well, not in the literal sense of . . . never mind. Check with Tom, he'll vouch that I'm an okay guy."

I looked over at Tom. Sonofabitch was standing there with the damn phone in his ear, hand over the receiver laughing, giving me the thumbs up. Pissed me off. I put my hand over the receiver and yelled across the room at Tom, "Hang up the phone, motherfucker, before I come over there, wrap the cord around your skinny little cock and string you up to the goddamn roof."

Tom laughed, "Sounds like fun, Mat. Saturday night maybe? Or is your dance card full?"

But he saw the "now, motherfucker" on my face and hung up the phone.

I put the receiver back up to my ear and said, "Edgar? Sorry, I'm back."

Edgar said, "What's going on up there?"

"Nothing," I said. "We've got rats in the woodwork. Just had to smash one."

"So? Did I pass inspection? Dinner tonight?"

I thought for a minute. Sweaty, scrungy, need a shower, tired. Me, not him. Said, "Nah, Edgar. Dinner, yeah. Tonight, no. How's Friday for you?"

"Friday's great, Mat! Pick you up here?" Edgar was clearly excited. Had a little good-puppy lilt in his voice.

"Here? No, Edgar, not here. Here is where I spend all day getting sweaty and filthy. Here is where there are a bunch of jerks who would just love me to give them any slight hint of my personal life to feed me a raft of shit about. Not here, Edgar."

"Okay, got it. Mum's the word, no one at your work shall know you are seeing the likes of such as me. I'll pick you up at your place. Seven-thirty on Friday. Where do you live?" Edgar rolled over on his back and showed me his belly.

Fuck. This guy had a couple of endearing qualities. Could be trouble. I gave him my address at The Egypt. Big godawful tacky pink building on top of the hill by the Burke Gilman Trail bike path. Can't miss it.

Nipples hungering for suck.

Friday rolled around and so did Edgar. Showed up at the front door all cleaned up. Me at the front door all cleaned up. Both of us sparkly a bit. We went to the new restaurant down on the wharf, Kali's Kachina. Waiters in loincloths, more guys in loincloths walking around playing flutes and telling stories. Short ones. The loincloths that is, not the stories. Some of the stories ran a little long and would have interfered with the conversation, had Edgar and I actually been having one. Had to pick all your food live out of the tank and have it killed on the spot. Drank lots of *grappa* and killed a couple lobsters and an angus for dinner.

Edgar was getting more endearing by the moment.

We went dancing after dinner. Across the lake at Hedge On The Dike. The band playing was Jazz Oneself. They were great. Lots of raunchy get-down-and-thrum-my-cunt-open deep bass and drum shit. Edgar could actually dance—actually appeared to love to dance. Edgar was almost to the top of the endearment scale. We renewed our dance-fucked bodies with a fair amount of Widmer beer between sets.

The *grappa* and the Widmer were finally starting to win. The band had clearly gone over the top and was on the downward slide. Edgar and I sat sharing one last beer. Edgar said, "So. What now? Am I going to get to touch that flat fucking beautiful body of yours tonight?"

Jeezus. Edgar was displaying some flat fucking full-on endearing qualities this fair eve. I said, "Yeah, Edgar, I think you're probably going to get to touch this flat fucking beautiful body of mine. And I think if that be true, it would be appropriate for us to blow this pop stand right about now."

We headed back to The Egypt. Headed back to the hot tub on the roof of the Egypt. No one was ever in the pink-tiled hot tub on the pink roof of The Egypt after dark, so I figured it would be a good place to do the starting-touching thing, to get Edgar's tongue in my mouth, to maybe get Edgar's cock in my mouth, to maybe get Edgar's mouth on my cunt. To get some of the preliminaries in the works before we got down to serious fucking.

Edgar was delighted with the pink-tiled hot tub on the pink roof of The Egypt. Edgar was delighted with me.

Asked me to keep on my tight red dancing dress until we got up there. Asked me to take it off for him in the shadow of a just-full moon. Asked me to take it off slow while he sat in a chair watching. I liked that.

I took my tight red dancing dress off. Slow. Laid it over the back of the pink chair on the pink-tiled roof. Enjoyed the good-sized rise in his pants when he saw the black bra that didn't have cups over my breasts. Just breasts, pulled up and pushed out by black silk-covered wires running down the outsides of my breasts, pushing up under the bottoms, meeting in the middle. Enjoyed the way his eyes defocused when he saw leather-looking black crotchless panties with a thong back. Enjoyed Edgar asking me to turn around. Slow. Enjoyed Edgar telling me to keep on my bra and panties. To get in the hot tub on the other side of him and bend over with my hands on the pink-tiled edge. Enjoyed waiting, hearing Edgar fumbling with his belt behind me, cussing at his shoes. Enjoyed hearing the little splash of Edgar's legs hitting the water. Enjoyed a lot, Edgar coming up behind me and slipping his hard into my wet. And out. And in. And out.

Really enjoyed Edgar's big dick. Enjoyed when I came hard. When Edgar came hard. When Edgar left his big dick inside me for just a couple minutes, me leaned all the way over the edge of the pink-tiled tub now with my hands on the edges of a pink chair. Enjoyed when Edgar was hard again inside me. Didn't enjoy when Edgar pulled out. Enjoyed when Edgar told me to turn around and take his cock in my mouth. His cock slippery with both of us. Enjoyed when I reached around Edgar and felt his silky ass.

Hated when I moved my hands further up Edgar's back to pull him in closer and felt hair. Long baboon hair.

That was the last time I saw Edgar.

MONDAY AFTERNOON

I am noticing that writers tend to get just a bit superstitious when things are going well. Like changing anything at all will make the story go away. Little things, like going inside to eat when we haven't eaten all day. Well, not eaten other than ginger animal cookies and dark chocolate raspberry sticks. Although we did add moderate quantities of beer to no great detriment. Little things like, well, the first time this morning I took a break for a cigarette, I popped some Kali Phos on the way back in, so I'd better do that each time I go back out for a cigarette. Little stuff like that.

I do understand that I'm making pretty general judgements on writers based on the direct experience of just two of that number. But I have a sneaking suspicion that those are fair global judgements.

So, gosh. I think that's the end of the hairy back stories. Although Mat did tell me a great shaved back story. Which probably wouldn't fit the context—such as it is—of The Novel particularly well at this point.

Man at 67, having become a woman, discovers he's a lesbian.

So I am sitting here, wanting to write the outsides of this story, this book, this Novel. And my body is just wanting this woman here in the room with me. Wanting her to quit typing. To turn around and tell me to quit typing. Wanting her to come over to this bed and lay me down and touch me hard. Soft. Deep.

I don't often make love with women. I do like the hardness, the aggressiveness, of men. And the yielding, the yielding into yielding, of woman on woman.

Oh yeah, that too.

I was somehow embarrassed by her slippery swollen open. It told me too much.

I get horny when I write. Well, not horny, exactly, not consciously. Maybe more of a tension deal, except not really.

I think that writing and dancing and sex all come from the same place in me, all run on the same energy. I didn't know that until a couple weeks ago. With all of them, my sex gets wet when I am in the flow of it. With all of them, the boundaries between are slim.

One of those things you don't even tell your friends. Unless of course you are writing something which is to end up at book length. And then you become progressively more willing to tell the entire world—or at least whatever minute percentage of the population of strangers in the world might ever read it—your deepest darkest secrets if they'll take up another few paragraphs of infinite white space.

We already are making love.

So this time has been hard. Hard to stay open enough to write full on with someone my body wants—I want—in the room, to not shield her from me and so shove my words out of my body. Shove me out of my body.

I am here now. All the way here. Not much caring about shielding this person. I get that she is strong enough to not need my shielding. I get that I am strong enough to stay out in the open without being irretrievably hurt.

The old news, she does die hard.

Mat and I thought about breaking for dinner. Decided not to. That would be eating, a change in the pattern of a good writing day. We came back inside and wrote some more.

My housemates started to barbecue dinner. Smelled like teriyaki salmon. Or maybe steak. Smelled great, even if it was steak, even though I'm a vegetarian.

Mat and I thought again about breaking for dinner. Decided dinner might be a good idea. Justified it by remembering we'd added beer to the day with no substantial visible effects.

We sat down to eat. Mu Shou and salad.

I said, "It looks like the table blew up the wind." My mouth's not working very well right now. Not sure if the short in the connection is beer or words.

Mat blesses her food before she eats. Mat's blessing this time was, "We eat our brains all day and now sit here asking you to fix it."

The sentence with the table and the wind was supposed to be, "It looks like the wind blew up the tablecloth."

Not much further into the meal I said, "This Mu Shou is hot." Good so far. Not a great sentence, but it is in English.

Mat said, "Yeah, but the time before that it was still cold in the middle when I checked it."

I said, "Whose finger did you stick it into?" And then stared at her blankly when she started laughing so hard she choked on her Mu Shou.

Then heard what I had said on the delayed playback mechanism and started laughing so hard I choked on my Mu Shou.

The sentence about the heat of the Mu Shou was supposed to be, "Whose Mu Shou did you stick your finger in?"

I am now extremely relieved that I can straighten these sentences out if I don't try to say them out loud.

Mat had stuck her finger in her own Mu Shou. She turned it over and showed me where she had cut her second Mu Shou open and inserted her finger.

There's more to the Mu Shou story. I'm certain you are fairly looking forward to hearing it, so I will tell it.

Mat was working on her second Mu Shou. She opened her mouth and pulled out a short blonde hair. Mat's hair is dark brown and short. My hair is light brown and long. Her dogs have short black hair. My dog has medium red hair.

Mat said, "There's a blonde hair in my Mu Shou. Which would seem to indicate that these Mu Shou were made by people of not Oriental origin. Oriental persons aren't blonde."

I said, "Well, this Mu Shou was from Trader Joe's. I think the package said, 'Made in L.A.' on it."

There was a wee bit of a pause while Mat continued to eat her Mu Shou and I waited to see if anything else would happen. I said, "Well, I'm impressed. Some people would get totally grossed out by a blonde hair showing up in their Oriental Mu Shou from Trader Joe's. Although I don't quite understand that, we put other people's pubic hair in our mouths deliberately. But for some reason it grosses a lot of people out to find one little head hair in their food."

Mat said, "That's ridiculous. We put other people's tongues in our mouths. Hair is a lot less gross than tongues."

91

I said, "Well, I don't know about that. I've seen some hair that was a lot grosser than any tongue I've ever had in my mouth. Well, maybe except for one. Doug Wall had an exceptionally gross tongue. As flabby as his cock."

There was a pause while Mat and I chomped on our Mu Shou.

I said, "Another great first sentence—There was a blonde hair in my Mu Shou . . ."

Mat said, "A blonde hair from a person of not Oriental origin. A blonde hair in my Mu Shou from Trader Joe's."

I picked up, "My Mu Shou from Trader Joe's. My Mu Shou with the blonde hair from a person of not Oriental origin. The blonde hair from my Mu Shou wrapped around my tongue."

Mat: "My tongue, that had been touching the Mu Shou. Now the blonde hair touching my tongue that had been touching the Mu Shou. My tongue, that had touched other tongues."

Me: "My tongue that touched the Mu Shou with the blonde hair from Trader Joe's. My tongue that had touched other hair. Other blonde hair. Other brown hair. Other black hair. Hair in other places than the Mu Shou from Trader Joe's."

Mat: "Hair in deep dark places between open thighs. Hair that had never seen a Mu Shou. Had never seen a Mu Shou from Trader Joe's. A Mu Shou from Trader Joe's with a blonde hair wrapped around my tongue."

Me: "My tongue that had been in deep dark places between open thighs. Thighs opened to my tongue. To my tongue with the last cold remains of Mu Shou. And one blonde hair."

Mat: "From Trader Joe's."

We both choked on our Mu Shou again. Laughing.

I don't know how to spell Mu Shou. Figure I'm going to have to go dig through the garbage and find the wrapper on the Mu Shou from Trader Joe's.

But just then, right about now, Ba, who is one of the little black dogs, one of Mat's dogs, comes trotting out of the other room with a Mu Shou wrapper in his mouth. A Mu Shou wrapper with the words "Mu Shou" somewhere in Ba's digestive tract. The microwave instructions are still intact. So is the nutritional breakdown. I still don't know how to spell Mu Shou.

Mat is going out for a cigarette. It has been ten minutes since the last one. That's a litttle short between cigarette breaks, but fuck it. Who's counting?

Mat going out for a cigarette meant it was time for Ba and Angus—Angus being the other little black dog of Mat's scotty dogs—to go outside. Mat opened the sliding glass door. Ba picked up speed and rammed full tilt into the screen door. Rammed his little black nose right into the wire mesh. I knew he couldn't see out from underneath the long black hair hanging over his little black eyes, had told Mat that. He's been here three days and I haven't seen his eyes yet.

Mat said, "See your shadow there on the door, Ba? That means it's a struc-ture."

I choked on my water. Laughing. Mat went out for a

cigarette. We're all somewhere on the far side of rummy as hell.

I didn't change the sheets for
a month after he left.

I said, "I feel like such a whore."

Mat didn't break from her typing. "Why?"

I said, "Because I'm just writing what's going on. All those Other People out there had outlines and notes and characters and actual Honest-To-God stories. And I sit here writing Mu Shou and Grandma and your stories."

Mat stopped typing. "Jesus, woman. What Other People? You're sitting here beating yourself up for writing what's up for you to write right now. Shut the fuck up and write."

I shut the fuck up and wrote.

I thought I knew once where to go,
what to do, who to love, how to be.

Three hours and eleven minutes of the allotted seventy-two to go. All I can say about that is thank you, God. Body's wiped, brain's gone, don't know why I ever fucking thought I could write anyway. Or why I thought I could write within the framework of this kind of structure. As if structure's my very best thing.

Speaking of which, this story has none at this moment. The transcribing/editing process is going to be like playing Writer's Scrabble. Cut the sucker apart and start moving pieces around until some sort of theoretical coherence appears. There is no apparent pattern from where I'm sitting right now. Making me nuts.

All that sparkles in my body
has been eaten, used up,
shit out.

Mat and I have been writing for thirteen hours with no breaks but for cigarettes.
Oh. And Mu Shou.

Thirteen hours writing hard. Easy. Having fun. Some good stuff in there. Maybe mostly good stuff. Form is another issue altogether.

Two hours and twenty-eight minutes to go. Feels like I need two days and twenty-eight hours. Seventy-two hours plus four. The beginning place plus four.

I feel grungy. Tired. Got to take a shower. Might wake me up. Will at least get rid of that greasy, stringy, grungy feeling.
Does that. Doesn't do a fucking thing to wake me up.

Maybe if I'd made it a cold shower. But I feel like I've flogged myself enough for one seventy-two hour period.

Started bleeding this morning. A week and a half early. Bleeding myself dry. Eating my brain. Shitting out words. Will have no body left to hold me if I don't stop. Soon.

Maybe a walk. The dogs are all chewing on themselves viciously. Stress reaction to closed quarters and too much company. Maybe moving my body will wake me up. Maybe strolling the dog will help her quit chewing before I knock her over the head with my laptop.

We walk. Mat brings her dogs, too. No words. We don't go as far as last night.

It doesn't help. One hour and twenty-eight minutes left. Mat says she needs to go home. Needs to sleep in her own bed. She has written through to the end of her story. Mat has a story, and an end. She goes.

I'm wiped. One hour and thirteen minutes left. Now twelve. Seventy-two minutes to finish. To know what it is that I need to say. The one thing. The one story. Feels like I have used up every ounce of all that is good in my body.

And somewhere between today and death
I will give up expecting

And softly whisper
Yes.

There is only one reason good enough to tell a story—to write a story—and that is because the storyteller needs to tell it.

Let it be so.

 MS. LOREE HARRELL is a thirty-six-year-old writer and editor who dropped out of the corporate business world to dedicate her time to writing. She is currently working on two short story collections: *Sex, Death and Other Odds & Ends* and *The Simplest Insanity*. She presently lives and works in Sandy, Oregon.

PAST 3-DAY NOVEL WINNERS

STOLEN VOICES/VACANT ROOMS
Steve Lundin & Mitch Parry
1993 double winner: 1-895636-06-X; $9.00

A CIRCLE OF BIRDS
Hayden Trenholm
1992 winner: 1-895636-03-5; $7.95

O FATHER: A Murder Mystery
Bill Dodds
1990 winner: 0-88978-229-6; $7.95

WASTEFALL
Stephen E. Miller
1989 winner: 0-88978-220-2; $7.95

PAWN TO QUEEN: A Chris Prior Mystery
Pat Dobie
1988 winner: 0-88978-209-1; $6.95

STARTING SMALL
James Dunn
1987 winner: 0-88978-195-8; $6.95

HARDWIRED ANGEL
Candas Jane Dorsey & Nora Abercrombie
1986 winner: 0-88978-190-7; $5.95

MOMENTUM
Marc Diamond
1985 winner: 0-88978-179-6; $5.95

NOTHING SO NATURAL
Jim Curry
1984 winner: 0-88978-167-2; $5.95

THIS GUEST OF SUMMER
Jeff Doran
1983 winner: 0-88978-151-6; $5.95

STILL
b.p. nichol
1982 winner: 0-88978-146-x; $4.95

ACCORDION LESSONS
Ray Serwylo
1981 winner: 088978-122-2; $4.95

DOCTOR TIN
Tom Walmsley
1979 winner—out of print